three little peas

To Fernand's and Marinette's green thumbs, and my thanks to Olivier, Marilda, Ju, Célie, and Jérémie

www.enchantedlion.com

First American edition published in 2014 by Enchanted Lion Books, 351 Van Brunt Street, Brooklyn, NY 11231
Translation Copyright © 2014 by Enchanted Lion Books
Translated from the French by Claudia Z. Bedrick
Originally published in France by éditions Rouergue Copyright © 2012 as *Trois petits pois*
All rights reserved under International and Pan-American Copyright Conventions
A CIP record is on file with the Library of Congress ISBN 978-1-59270-155-1
Printed in March 2014 in China by South China Printing Company

marine rivoal

three little peas

ENCHANTED LION BOOKS

NEW YORK

The garden is beginning to bloom.

Two little peas pop out
to get some air.

They are round.

They are green.

They go here...

...and there.

They go up!

They go
under.

They try new things.

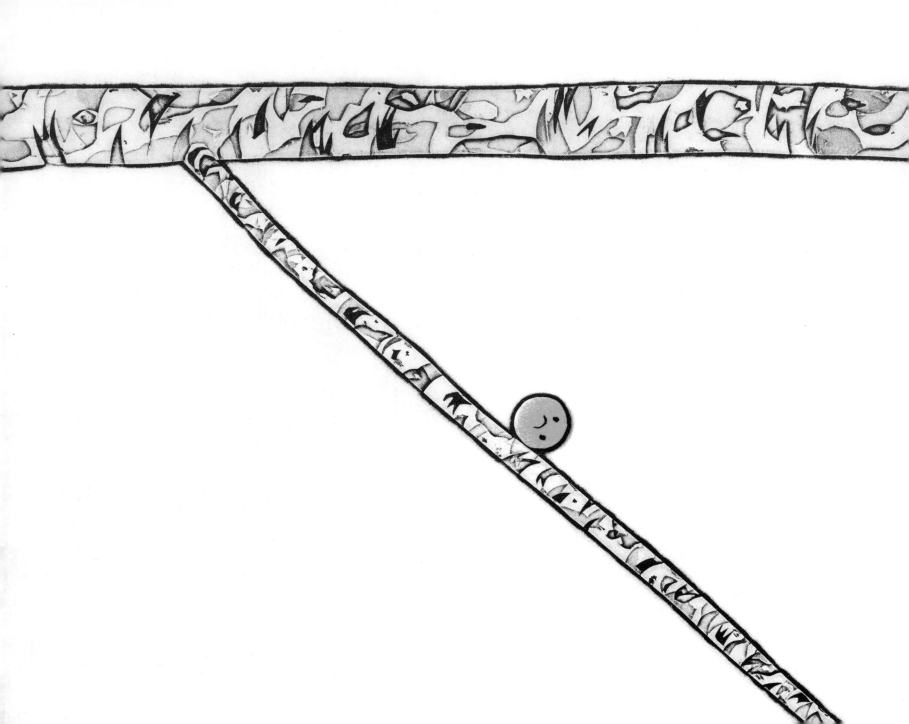

Oh! How high they are.

Now they have come down.

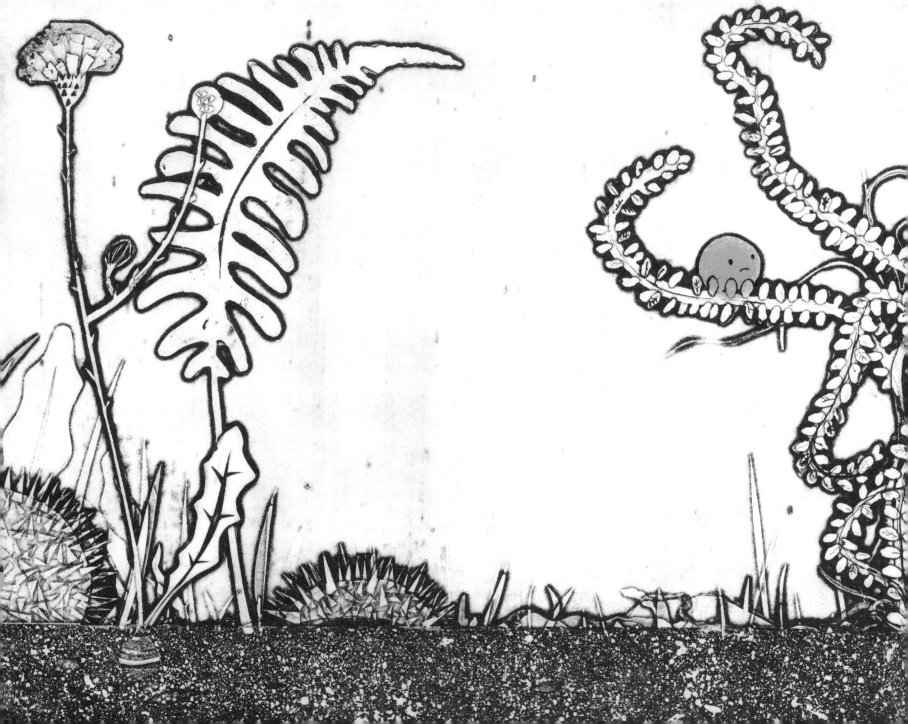

Look! How did they
get up there?

Oh, dear! Oh, dear!
Save those peas!

Two little peas bounce and roll,
speeding up as they go.

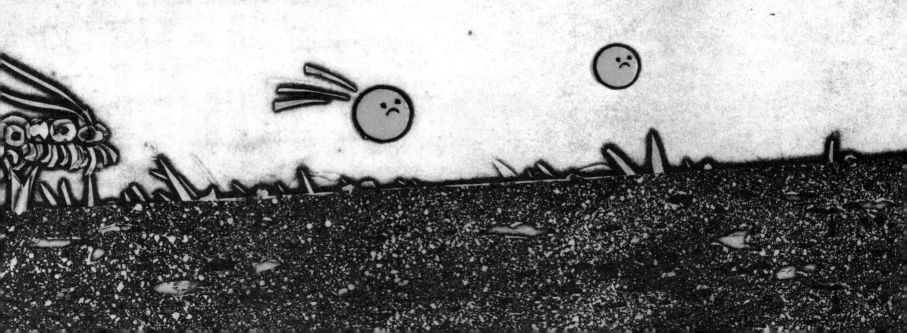

They end up in a safe place.

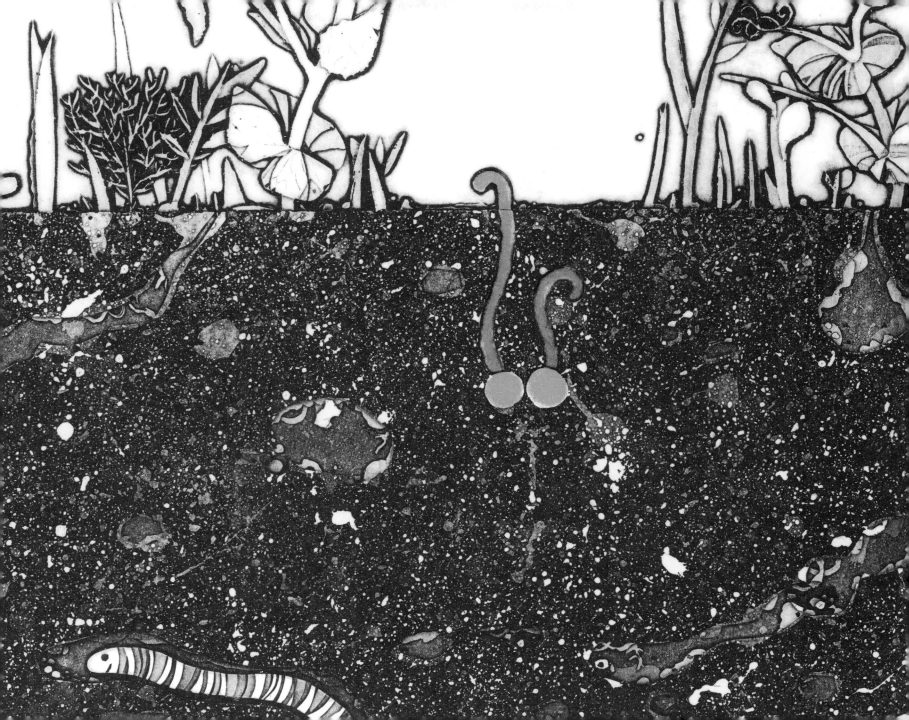

And this little pea makes three!

Engravers Association Studio

Ink spatulas

Adding, removing, and repositioning tape before another acid bath

Adding, removing, and repositioning tape before another acid bath

Zinc plate and the print pulled from that plate

Zinc plate and the print pulled from that plate

About the illustrations

To create the illustrations in this book, Marine Rivoal used an old technique called etching, but she used this technique in her own way.

Like all etchers, Marine works on a metal plate—a zinc plate in her case, rather than a copper one. But she doesn't work as etchers normally do by varnishing the plate, drawing with a metal point on the varnish, and then plunging the plate into an acid bath, where the drawn lines are bit, or etched, into the plate. Instead, Marine places pieces of tape over parts of her plate. She then draws on the tape with a scalpel, almost as if her technique was that of cut paper. After she has finished her drawing, made by cutting shapes and lines into the tape, Marine puts her plate into the acid bath. The nitric acid of the bath eats away at the plate wherever it isn't covered by the tape, so its surface becomes very much like a bas-relief, with dug-out areas and raised surfaces.

Marine goes through the process of adding pieces of tape, moving others, and removing some altogether several times for each plate, and each time she uses her scalpel to draw on the tape before putting the plate back into the acid bath. Once Marine has decided that she has the surfaces and depths on her plate that she needs for the picture to look the way she wants it to, she removes all of the tape and inks the plate. She does this by hand, using a small piece of cloth to get the ink into the grooves. Any excess ink is removed with newspaper. The inking spatulas are used only for mixing different shades of black ink together to achieve the right tone. Because Marine inks the plate by hand, her fingers are always black.

Once the plate has been inked, it is ready for printing. Marine then places the plate on to the bed of the press and puts a damp piece of paper over it. Full of suspense, she turns the crank, eager to see what the result will be. The image that she discovers on the paper is the same as the picture on the plate, except it is reversed.

It is the inked lines themselves that create suspense, and what Marine is waiting to see are the shades of black that result. The light grays, medium grays, and deep blacks in the prints that make up the illustrations in this book are the result of the shallowness or depth of the lines, for it is this variation that determines how the ink will print on to the paper.

Marine loves every step involved in making pictures this way. It's a bit complicated, rather like putting together a big puzzle with small pieces, but it's challenging and really satisfying. Marine describes her job as an etcher as similar to being a chemist or a cook. Rigor and technique matter a lot, but chance and innovation do too. Interesting, unexpected things happen all the time, and Marine is often pleasantly surprised by the outcome.

Marine Rivoal at work at the Engravers Association Studio

About Marine Rivoal

Born in the French countryside in 1987, Marine Rivoal quickly moved with her family to Paris, where she spent a happy childhood. After receiving her baccalauréat, Marine went to art school, where she threw herself into learning everything she could about the art and craft of bookmaking. In 2008, she received her second degree, this time in graphic arts, from the Estienne Art School. Next, she went to the School of Decorative Arts in Strasbourg, from which she graduated in 2011. There she deepened her skills and knowledge of engraving and began to experiment with different printing techniques. In 2012, she published her first book—*Three Little Peas* (*Trois petits pois* in French)—with éditions du Rouergue. That same year, she also began a film with Claire Sichez and Xbo Films. Today, Marine continues her experiments and projects at the ETR Balistic Studio, a collective for printing and engraving on the outskirts of Paris.